TANTRI THE MANTRI
GAME OF A THRONE

Welcome, my future subjects, to this collection of stories about me, me and me! In these pages, you will see my cunning and my charm, my wit and my wickedness…. and all the qualities that make a great ruler. If Hujli were a democracy, you would have certainly voted for me as your leader. But, until that happens, I must keep trying to get the throne, so that my immense talents are not eclipsed by Hooja's equally immense belly (Sigh). In fact, my determination to get to the throne speaks highly of my strength of character. But don't go on my word alone. Look at what my fans have to say about me… and my comments in the brackets.

Readers Speak:

"Tantri the Mantri is always outstanding." – **Sudeshna Ausali** *(Hear Hear!)*

"Evil though Tantri is, he does make me laugh." – **Tapasmi Ray Chaudhuri** *(I don't know what's so funny about my evil-ness.)*

"Tantri the Mantri my old-time favourite. And he has changed into something literally awesome!" – **Danie Joseph, Bahrain** *(Old! Who is she calling old?)*

"I am a big fan of Tantri. I like him when he makes a death trap for king Hooja." – **Niranjan Marde** *(Ah! Maybe I should hire him to be my next Dushtabuddhi.)*

"I like Tantri the Mantri because every time Tantri tries to kill Hooja, his plan fails and he has to run away! The stories are thrilling." – **Anaica Ramesh,** *Navi Mumbai* *(I don't run away! I just take a step back to plan better.)*

Now, get to reading so that you can do some praising of your own. And there are some brand new content pages in this book… your future king's gift to you. Enjoy! And if you like what you read, write to me at tinklemail@ack-media.com

The Hidden Cave	3
The Pharaoh's Walk	8
The Prisoner A-Zenda	12
Royal Makeover	19
The Royal Wish List	20
Hooja's Buddy	22
April Fool!	27
The Haunted Palace	32
Following the Signs	39
The Prick of the Purple Yen	40
The Foolproof Plan	47
Mantris and More	51
Fish Pond	53
The Assassin	60
Clone Mania	64

Tantri the Mantri
The Hidden Cave

Writer: R. Nalini
Illustrator: Prachi Killekar
Colourist: Umesh Sarode

"THE ROCKS OF THE HIDDEN CAVE ON ZARGOI ISLAND GIVE OUT POISONOUS FUMES..."

"...MANY UNWARY EXPLORERS HAVE PERISHED IN THE CAVES IN THE LAST FEW DECADES..."

INTERESTING! VERY NTERESTING!

COINCIDENTALLY, HOOJA IS BUILDING A ROCK GARDEN. PERHAPS I COULD... YES, YES, IT'S A GREAT IDEA!

YOU THINK WE SHOULD GO TO THE ZARGOI ISLAND IN SEARCH OF ROCKS FOR MY GARDEN?

THAT'S RIGHT, YOUR MAJESTY!

I'VE HEARD THERE ARE RARE ROCKS IN THE CAVE ON ZARGOI ISLAND... YOUR MAJESTY COULD HANDPICK A FEW ROCKS...

THAT'S FANTASTIC! MAKE ARRANGEMENTS FOR THE TRIP.

WE'LL LEAVE NEXT WEEK!

ROCKING!

* An Ancient Egyptian Sun God

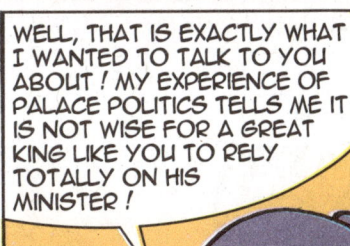

Royal Makeover

Well, the truth is… I need a makeover for when I become king. How about trying your hand at lending tasteful colours to these new clothing styles? And while you're at it, you can pick out new moustache styles (some are given as suggestions) to suit my royal (and handsome) face. Of course, you can try out more clothing and moustache styles for me in your sketchbook. And make sure, I look royally good. Or else…

Text: Dolly Pahlajani   Illustration: Vineet Nair   Layout: Jitendra Patil

The Royal Wish List

WELL, EVERY GREAT KING NEEDS A BEAUTIFUL THRONE AND A CROWN THAT WILL BE THE ENVY OF ALL OTHER RULERS. AND I HAVE COMPILED A WISH LIST OF WHAT I WANT WHEN I BECOME KING OF HUJLI. AND SINCE THE LIST IS REALLY LONG, I'M SHARING JUST THE HIGHLIGHTS HERE.

The Peacock Throne
The most famous throne of all time and what a magnificent epitome of workmanship! Designed for the Mughal Emperor Shah Jahan, this throne stood on golden feet, set with precious stones. Two open peacock tails formed the backrest and they were gilded, enamelled and inset with the most gorgeous jewels known to humankind, including the Koh-i-noor, the largest known diamond. And to access the throne, the king had to climb a set of silver steps. What richness! Any king would covet it on sight. No wonder Nader Shah, the Persian ruler who invaded India, stole the Peacock Throne. And after his assassination, the throne was dismantled and it simply disappeared! Vanished into thin air! And the jewels somehow made their way to Britain where they are the pride of the royal regalia.

The Crown of Queen Elizabeth
So what if this crown was designed for a queen? It will look grand on a king's head too (my head, in case anyone was wondering). Designed for the coronation of Queen Elizabeth (Wife of King George VI) in 1937, this crown is made of platinum and is inset with the Koh-i-noor (Unfortunately, they had to cut the diamond to fit it into the crown. Sigh.) and other precious jewels. Presently, it is kept on display in the Jewel House at the Tower of London, a fortress that's now a tourist attraction.

Text: Dolly Pahlajani   Illustration: Vineet Nair   Colours: Umesh Sarode   Layout: Jitendra Patil

Naderi Throne
'Nader' is a Persian word meaning 'rare' or 'unique', and the Naderi throne sure lives up to its name. Designed for the Shah of Iran, Fat'h Ali Shah Qajar (1772–1834), this throne was portable and could be divided into 12 separate parts so that the Shah could take it with him to his summer residences. The throne is made of wood that is covered with gold and encrusted with almost 26,000 jewels! What opulence it must have seen in its days! Today, the throne is kept safe in the national treasury of the Central Bank of Iran. Maybe, if I get my hands on it, it can relive its glory days again.

Imperial Crown of Russia
Also known as the Great Imperial Crown, this stunning piece was used by the rulers of Russia until monarchy ended in 1917. The crown was made in 1762 for the coronation of Catherine the Great, the longest-ruling female leader of Russia. It is adorned by almost 5000 diamonds, and bordered by lines of pearls. And it is encrusted with the second-largest spinel in the world, said to have been brought in from China. The crown is Russia's pride and has been included in the National Emblem of the Russian Federation. Currently, it has been kept out of my reach in the Kremlin Armoury in Moscow.

The Diamond Throne
Several thrones belonging to Russian Tsars are stored in the Kremlin in Moscow. Among these, the most elaborate one is the diamond armchair belonging to the Tsar Alexei Mikhailovich (1629–1676). The throne was made by Persian craftsmen using sandalwood covered with gold and silver plates bearing exquisite carving. And like its name, the throne has about 876 diamonds on its surface along with 1,223 other precious stones. On the back of the throne, there is an embroidered Latin inscription that glorifies the Tsar and his powers. What more does a king want?

Crown of Saint Wenceslas
This crown I crave simply for the legend associated with it. I will tell you all about it, but let me introduce you to the crown first.

The Crown of Saint Wenceslas was designed in 1347 for the 11th Bohemian king, the Holy Roman Emperor Charles IV, who dedicated it to the patron saint of the country, St. Wenceslas. Wrought from 22 karat gold and decorated with pearls, sapphires, emeralds, and other precious stones, this crown was used for the coronation of all Bohemian* Kings. An old Czech legend says that anyone who dares to usurp the throne and wear this crown is doomed and shall die within a year. Now, I simply need to convince Hooja to do just that. Muhaha!

Belonging to Bohemia, a historical country which is now a part of Czech Republic

Tantri The Mantri
April Fool!

Writer: L. Prabhu
Illustrator: Prachi Killekar
Colourist: Rajesh Phatak

FOLLOWING THE SIGNS

Text: Dolly Pahlajani Layout: Jitendra Patil

Take this pop quiz to find out whether you have it in you to follow in my crooked footsteps and aim for the throne. That does not mean you can rule *my* Hujli (find your own).

1. You and your friends are out for dinner. There's a last slice of pizza left on the table. You…
a. try to convince the others that the last slice has curdled and is unfit for consumption but you're ready to sacrifice yourself for the sake of their health
b. lick your fingers before offering the piece to others
c. grab it before you've finished eating the slice you have. It's best to plan for the future.

2. You've forgotten to do your homework. You…
a. put on your puppy face and try to wag your way out of punishment
b. snatch your neighbour's homework and threaten to set your pet lizard on him/her if they complain
c. try to convince the teacher that you're above such insignificant things as homework

3. You want water but are too tired to fetch it yourself. You…
a. devise a robot to do it for you. But by the time it's done, you're dehydrated enough to need medical attention
b. bribe your sibling to get it for you
c. bribe your sibling to get it for you but use fake notes (which look as good as real ones) to pay him/her

4. You're playing a game. You…
a. usually win by fair means
b. have an arrangement with the referee/umpire/judge to call the game in your favour
c. have clones of you playing on the field. That way, you always win.

5. You take your dog out for a walk. Who leads?
a. The dog
b. You
c. Why would you even walk your own dog? Get someone else to do it.

6. Your class loses a quiz because of you. You…
a. look for people to pass the blame on to
b. put on a tragic show and end up making your classmates console you and promise to do your homework for a week
c. hire a group of hypnotists and wipe all their memories clean

The Moment of Truth:
As: You are too simple-minded and unfit to show your face in the royal courts. You could maybe pass off as a mir like Dushtabuddhi.
Bs: Ah, ambitious, aren't we? That's good. I like ambition. It reminds me of me. You'd make a good mantri, but you have a long way to go.
Cs: Greetings, Your (future) Highness! You have all the imperiousness and the cunning you need to aim for the th Now, just pray you don't have a mantri like me. Muhahaha!

"OF COURSE, SIR! FOLLOW ME."

"I KEEP MY 'WAR-STRATEGY' INGREDIENTS IN THERE."

"THE PURPLE YEN POISON. VERY, VERY FATAL!"

"INTERESTING!"

"A SINGLE PRICK WITH THE LIQUID CAN CAUSE INSTANT DEATH."

"WHAT ARE YOU DOING?! ARE YOU RAVING MAD?!"

"HEY, YOU SAID INSTANT DEATH... BUT I DON'T FEEL ANYTHING ODD."

"THAT'S THE SECRET OF THE PURPLE YEN. THE POISON IS ACTIVATED ONLY WHEN IT IS MIXED WITH A PINCH OF COMMON SALT. OTHERWISE, THE LIQUID IS AS SAFE AS WATER."

Mantris and More

LIKE PLAYING A BACKGROUND DANCER, NO MATTER HOW HARD YOU WORK AND HOW GRACEFULLY YOU DANCE, THE LIMELIGHT IS FOREVER TRAINED ON THE SUPERSTAR IN THE CENTRE. YET, THERE ARE A FEW OF US WHO'VE MANAGED TO STEAL THE SPOTLIGHT AND MAKE A NAME FOR OURSELVES. PRESENTING... THE MOST INTELLIGENT AND RENOWNED MANTRIS THAT OUR COUNTRY HAS EVER KNOWN (AFTER ME, OF COURSE).

Chanakya

Who hasn't heard of this smart gentleman from the Mauryan Empire? Also known as Kautilya or Vishnugupta, Chanakya served two generations of emperors—Chandragupta and his son, Bindusara. In fact, when Chandragupta ascended to the throne at a young, tender age, it was Chanakya who handled everything. This genius of ruling behind the ruler is amazing! No wonder Chanakya is considered one of the wisest ministers to have ever lived. A master at politics and economics, his book 'Arthashastra' is considered a pathbreaker even today.

Birbal

Now here's a gem... literally. Raja Birbal (at least he had the word 'Raja' in his title!) was one of the *Navratnas* or nine gems at the court of that great Mughal ruler, Emperor Akbar.

Birbal's real name was Mahesh Das and he had joined Akbar's court as a poet and singer but gained the emperor's favour because of his famous wit and intelligence. It was this legendary intelligence that has immortalized Birbal in several folktales. And even though he never really got to be king, I think he was pretty influential as a mantri.

Hyder Ali

Here's a man who does my heart good. For he is a mantri who became a ruler and made his son (remember the legendary Tipu Sultan?) a king too. Hyder Ali joined the military of Mysore's king, Krishnaraja Wodeyar II and soon became commander-in-chief of the king's army. After that, it was really easy to overthrow the king and declare himself sultan of Mysore. Pretty neat, huh? I want to follow in his foootsteps!

Text: Dolly Pahlajani Illustration: Vineet Nair
Colours: Umesh Sarode Layout: Jitendra Patil

SUBSCRIBE NOW!

TINKLE MAGAZINE		TINKLE DIGEST		TINKLE COMBO MAGAZINE + DIGEST	
1 yr subscription	2 yr subscription	1 yr subscription	2 yr subscription	1 yr subscription	2 yr subscription
Pay only ₹4̶8̶0̶ **₹380!**	Pay only ₹9̶6̶0̶ **₹750!**	Pay only ₹7̶2̶0̶ **₹580!**	Pay only ₹1̶4̶4̶0̶ **₹1080!**	Pay only ₹1̶2̶0̶0̶ **₹880!**	Pay only ₹2̶4̶0̶0̶ **₹1680!**

I would like a subscription for

TINKLE MAGAZINE ☐ 1 yr ☐ 2 yrs | **TINKLE COMBO** ☐ 1 yr ☐ 2 yrs | **TINKLE DIGEST** ☐ 1 yr ☐ 2 yrs

(Please tick the appropriate box)

YOUR DETAILS*

Name: .... Date of Birth: |__|__| / |__|__| / |__|__|__|__|

Address: ....

.... City: .... Pin: |__|__|__|__|__|__| State: ....

School: .... Class: ....

Tel: .... Mobile: + 91 - |__|__|__|__|__|__|__|__|__|__|

Email: .... Signature: ....

PAYMENT OPTIONS

☐ Cheque /DD:

Please enclose Cheque /DD no. |__|__|__|__|__|__| drawn in favour of 'ACK Media Direct Ltd.'

at .... (bank) for the amount .... ,

dated |__|__| / |__|__| / |__|__|__|__| and send it to: IBH Books & Magazines Distributers Pvt. Ltd., Arch No. 30, West Approach, Below Mahalaxmi Bridge, Mahalaxmi (W), Mumbai - 400034.

☐ Pay Cash on Delivery: Pay cash on delivery of the first issue to the postman. (Additional charge of ₹50 applicable)

☐ Pay by money order: Pay by money order in favour of "ACK Media Direct Ltd."

☐ Online subscription: Please visit: www.amarchitrakatha.com

For any queries or further information: Email: customerservice@ack-media.com or Call: 022-40497435 / 36

TANTRI THE MANTRI
FISH POND

Writer: L. Prabhu
Illustrator: Prachi Killekar
Colourist: Umesh Sarode

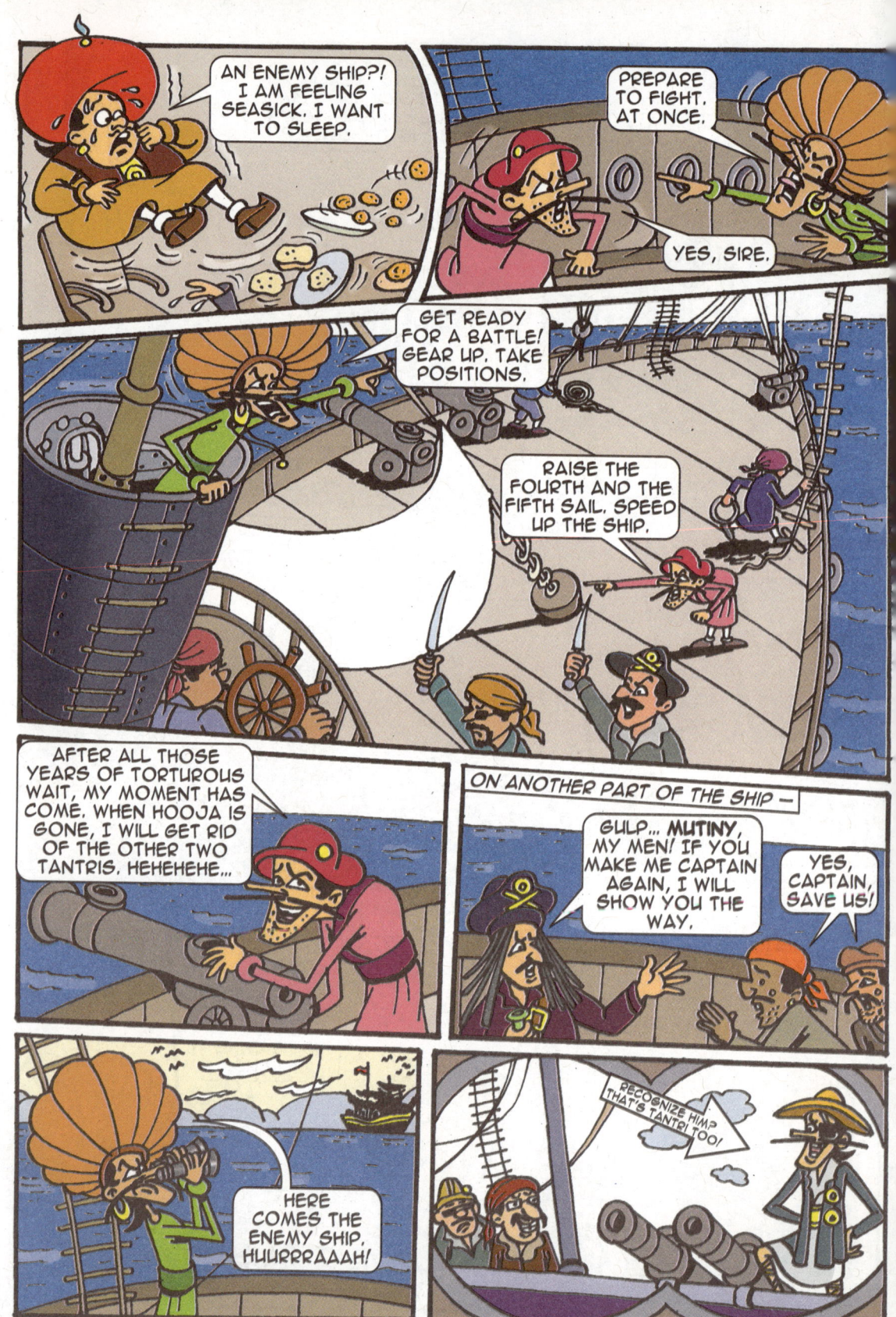